THE
STONEHOOK
SCHOONER

WRITTEN AND ILLUSTRATED BY JUDITH CHRISTINE MILLS

KPk
Key Porter Kids

Text and illustrations Copyright © 1995 by Judith Christine Mills

Canadian Cataloguing in Publication Data

Mills, Judith Christine
The stonehook schooner

ISBN 1-55013-653-4

I. title.

PS8576.I55S8 1995   jC813'.54   C95-931004-5
PZ7.M55St 1995

The publisher gratefully acknowledges the assistance of the Canada Council, the Ontario Publishing Centre and the Government of Ontario.

Key Porter Books Limited
70 The Esplanade
Toronto, Ontario
Canada M5E 1R2

Printed and bound in Hong Kong

95 96 97 98 99 5 4 3 2 1

FOR SAM

Each year, just as the last snow was melting
in the hills, Matthew helped his father
get the large, white schooner, the *Hannah
May*, ready for work.

All spring and summer and well into
the fall, Matthew's father and his crew
raked stones from the bottom of the
great lake, piled them in the hold, and
sold them in the big towns on the other
shore. It was hard work, and dangerous;
but the stonehookers were proud of their
skill. Their stones were paving broad
streets and building grand houses.

And each year, as Matthew and his father patched the hull of the
Hannah May, mended her huge sails, repaired her lines and ropes, and tied
down all her equipment, Matthew asked the same question.

"This year I'll be a stonehooker, too, won't I, Father? This year I'll see the big towns."

But his father always said, "You must be patient, Matthew. You are still too small. There will be plenty of time for you to go stonehooking."

Each time he said it, Matthew's father patted Matthew's shoulder sadly, as if to apologize. For Matthew would never be a stonehooker like his father and grandfather.

So many large stones had been raked from the shallows of the lake that few remained. And now there were quarries in the hills, where men cut stones and sent them speeding to the towns on the new fast railway. People in the towns could build their houses and roads without the stones from the lake.

Soon there would be no work for schooners like the *Hannah May*. Soon only the fine carpenters and a few sailors in the village would have jobs. Captain Adams had already left stonehooking. Now he was building sleek racing yachts for the rich people in the towns.

One day, as summer drew to a close, Matthew's father saw his son looking longingly at the boat, and said, "Hop aboard, Matthew. Today you can watch the stonehookers work."

Matthew's father had decided this would be the last season for the *Hannah May*, and he wanted Matthew to have a day on the schooner before it was too late. They would anchor in a shallow, protected cove where there were still a few large stones to harvest.

"Are we going to town?" Matthew asked excitedly.

"'Red sky in the morning, sailors take warning,' remember?" his father said, pointing at the red and pink flecks around the morning sun. "We should be safe enough in the cove, but it's no day to cross the open water."

Once the *Hannah May* was at anchor in the cove, the stone-hookers poled a small scow to shore. They waded into the cold water and raked the bottom of the lake until the iron tines of their

stonehooks caught on a large stone. They pried the stone loose
and dragged it through the water to the scow. Back and forth they
went until the scow was full of rocks.

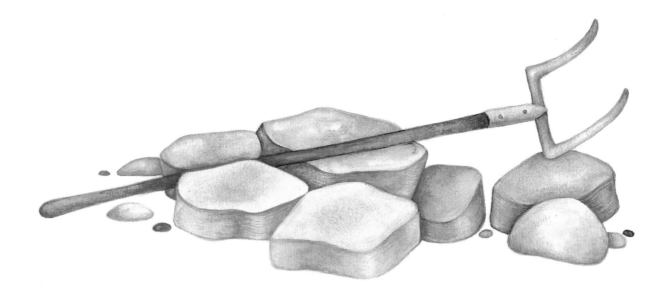

They poled the scow back to the *Hannnah May* and unloaded the heavy stones on deck. Then they carried them down into the hold. When the hold was full, they piled more rocks on the deck, carefully, so the *Hannah May* would be balanced and safe on her homeward run.

Late in the afternoon the wind shifted
to the north, and huge swells ran down
the lake. Thunder rumbled and cracked
around the *Hannah May*, and rain
drummed on the deck. Matthew's father
shouted to the stonehookers to wait out
the storm safely on shore.

Just as the last man scrambled up the
rocky bank, a huge wall of wind spun
the *Hannah May* around and pointed her
toward the mouth of the cove. The
anchor chain groaned and strained against
the heavily laden boat. Suddenly the
schooner was slammed broadside by a
huge wave, and the anchor chain snapped.

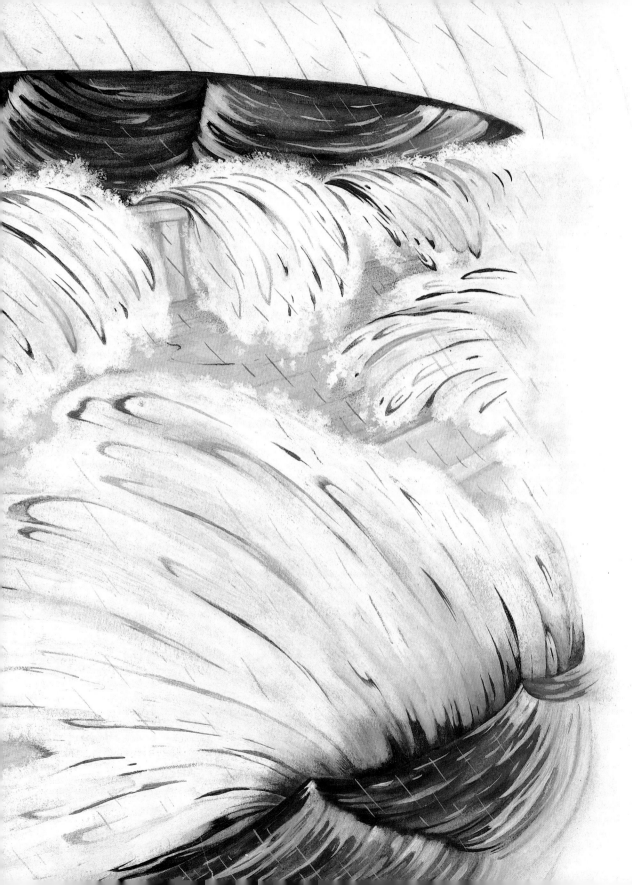

Matthew's father quickly ran up the storm jib so he could steer. He pulled on the wheel as hard as he could, but the wind and waves were too strong. The *Hannah May* rolled and pitched in the thick, dark soup of sky and water.

The rocks on the deck rolled from side to side, slamming against the wooden hull. Matthew's father shouted, "Stay close to me! We'll have to ride it out."

But Matthew scrambled toward the bow. He had to sight for land.
He quickly tied one end of a rope around his waist and the other end
to a mast. Then he squeezed into the point of the bow and crawled
forward as far as he could, squinting against the stinging rain and wind.
They might run aground and break up on the rocky shore, but it was
even more dangerous in the wild open water of the lake.

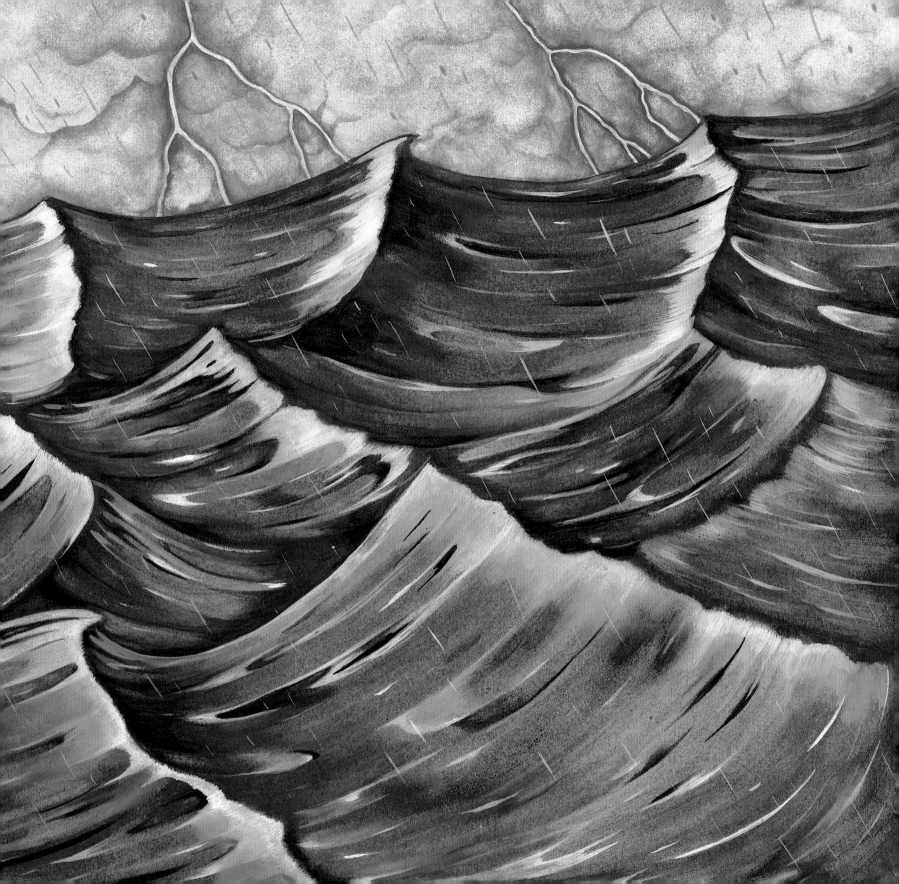

Finally, Matthew thought he saw a smudge of white. Could it be? Yes!
It was the warehouse by the dock. They had found their way home!
Matthew waved his arms and shouted, "This way! This way!"

Matthew's father put all his weight to the wheel and gradually turned the boat toward shore.

As often happens on that great lake, the storm rushed past as suddenly as it had hit, and Matthew's father guided the *Hannah May* safely into port.

As they docked, Captain Adams came out to meet them. "An impressive bit of navigating, young man," he said, and turned to Matthew's father. "Mr. Cutler, he shows great initiative, your lad. He would be a first-rate apprentice in my shipyard, and a fine yacht captain one day. He can start tomorrow, if you agree."

Matthew's father shook Captain Adams' hand. Then he smiled down at Matthew. "It will have to be the day after, Captain Adams. Tomorrow Matthew and I have a load of stones to take to town. It should be a fine day for a sail."

"'Red sky at night, sailors' delight,' Captain Adams," Matthew grinned, pointing to the streaks of rose and gold around the setting sun.

Historical Note

For almost one hundred years the stonehooking trade
flourished in the Lake Ontario ports of Port Credit, Oakville,
Bronte and Frenchman's Bay. Stonehookers would collect
chunks of Dundas shale, sand and gravel from the shallows of
the coves and transport them to cities such as Hamilton,
Toronto, Oswego and Rochester. There they were sold for use
in the construction of buildings, roads and breakwaters.

During the 1800s, more than one hundred such schooners
sailed back and forth across the lake. Many stonehookers were
lost to fierce lake storms, and tales abound of brave sailors and
daring rescues. By the early 1900s, however, improvements to
inland quarrying and the introduction of concrete for building
brought about the end of the stonehooking trade.